A Note to Parents and Caregivers:

Read-it! Readers are for children who are just starting on the amazing road to reading. These beautiful books support both the acquisition of reading skills and the love of books.

The RED LEVEL presents familiar topics using common words and repeating sentence patterns.

The BLUE LEVEL presents new ideas using a larger vocabulary and varied sentence structure.

The YELLOW LEVEL presents more challenging ideas, a broad vocabulary, and wide variety in sentence structure.

The GREEN LEVEL presents more complex ideas, an extended vocabulary range, and expanded language structures.

When sharing a book with your child, read in short stretches, pausing often to talk about the pictures. Have your child turn the pages and point to the pictures and familiar words. And be sure to reread favorite stories or parts of stories.

There is no right or wrong way to share books with children. Find time to read with your child, and pass on the legacy of literacy.

Adria F. Klein, Ph.D.
Professor Emeritus
California State University
San Bernardino, California

Editor: Bob Temple
Creative Director: Terri Foley
Editorial Adviser: Andrea Cascardi
Copy Editor: Laurie Kahn
Designer: Melissa Voda
Page production: The Design Lab
The illustrations in this book were painted with watercolor.

Picture Window Books
5115 Excelsior Boulevard
Suite 232
Minneapolis, MN 55416
1-877-845-8392
www.picturewindowbooks.com

Printed in the United States of America.

Library of Congress Cataloging-in-Publication Data
White, Mark, 1971–
The tortoise and the hare : a retelling of Aesop's fable / written by Mark White ;
illustrated by Sara Rojo.
p. cm. — (Read-it! readers fairy tales)
Summary: Recounts the famous tale of the race between the persevering turtle
and the boastful rabbit.
ISBN 1-4048-0215-0 (Hard Cover)
[1. Folklore. 2. Fables.] I. Aesop. II. Rojo, Sara, 1973– ill. III. Title. IV. Series.
PZ8.2.W55To 2004
398.2—dc21   2003006301

PICTURE WINDOW BOOKS

10/03

Read-it! Readers
Yellow Level

The Tortoise and the Hare
A Retelling of Aesop's Fable

Written by Mark White

Illustrated by Sara Rojo

Library Adviser:
Kathy Baxter, M.A.
Former Coordinator of Children's Services
Anoka County (Minnesota) Library

Reading Advisers:
Adria F. Klein, Ph.D.
Professor Emeritus, California State University
San Bernardino, California

Susan Kesselring, M.A.
Literacy Educator
Rosemount-Apple Valley-Eagan (Minnesota) School District

Picture Window Books
Minneapolis, Minnesota

One sunny morning, a tortoise decided to go for a walk.

Not long after the tortoise set out,
a hare passed him.

"Good morning," the hare said.
"I'm off to visit my sister."

When the hare came back after his visit, he saw the tortoise again. The tortoise had not moved very far. "Are you still way back here?" the hare asked.

"You may run as fast as the wind,"
the tortoise said, "but I bet I can
beat you in a race."

The next morning, the tortoise and the hare met and began their race.

The tortoise dragged himself forward.
The hare leaped and bounded
toward the finish line.

After a few minutes, the hare looked back over his shoulder. He could no longer see the tortoise.

The hare laughed to himself.
"This race will be so easy to win!"

Since he was so far ahead, the hare decided to stop and have a snack.

He crunched on some wild carrots.
He munched on some ripe, red
strawberries.

There was still no sign of the tortoise.
"It will take him forever to catch up to me,"
the hare said to himself. "I think I'll take
a quick nap in the shade."

The tortoise kept moving along.
He moved at a slow but steady pace.

Eventually, the tortoise came to the place where the hare was sleeping. Still, he didn't stop. He kept moving toward the finish line.

When the hare woke up from his nap,
he looked toward the starting line to see
if the tortoise was catching up.
There was still no sign of the tortoise.

The hare stretched and yawned.
Then he looked toward the finish line.
The tortoise was almost there!

22

The hare raced to catch up with the tortoise, but it was too late. The tortoise crossed the finish line first.

"You may run faster than I do, but I didn't give up," the tortoise said. "Sometimes, slow and steady wins the race."